My Love Is All Around

by
Danielle McLean

Illustrated by
Sebastien Braun

tiger tales

High on their hilltop,
Mommy and Baby Bear
looked down at the world below.

"We're so lucky," said Mommy Bear. "The sun is shining, and we're surrounded by love. We're the luckiest bears alive!"

"Is there really love all around us?" asked Baby Bear.

"Come on, little one—I'll show you . . . ."

Mommy and Baby Bear followed the winding stream. Baby Bear swung into Mommy's arms, squealing with excitement.

"Love is here right now," laughed Mommy. "It's in the butterflies fluttering above. It's in the games we play."

"Is it in the sun?" asked Baby Bear.
"Yes," replied Mommy.
"Whenever you feel the warmth
of the sun, you'll feel my love."

"And what about the birds?" questioned Baby Bear.
Mommy chuckled. "Love is definitely there
in the birdsong."
"I can hear something else, Mommy. Is that love, too?"

Mommy and Baby Bear followed
the noises to the grassy field, where
a family of rabbits was laughing
and bouncing.

"That sounds like love," said Baby Bear.
"It's the happiest sound I can think of."
"That's definitely love," agreed Mommy.
"They're giggling, just like we do!"

"But sometimes love is quiet, too," Mommy
continued. "Love can be as quiet as a whisper.
Shhh, my baby . . . can you hear?"

Baby Bear listened. There wasn't a sound!
Nothing but silence as the bears sat
close together, the afternoon sun
warming their fur.

Through the meadow came two foxes.
"Do you see that?" asked Mommy,
pointing to the fox kissing her cub.
"That's another way we show our love."

"You kiss me all the time!" exclaimed Baby Bear. "I must be SOOO loved!"

"What else does love look like?"
asked Baby Bear. "Is it when I
help my friends?"

"Of course!" replied Mommy. "There's
always love in kindness."
"You help me all the time," said
Baby Bear with a warm feeling
in his tummy.

"Where else is love, Mommy?" asked Baby
Bear. "Is it up on the hill?"
"Let's find out," answered Mommy, smiling.

The bears looked over at two deer sleeping
in the shimmering moonlight.
"That must be love," said Baby Bear.
"Just like when you cuddle me."

"And look up, my baby," added Mommy. "The stars are twinkling, full of love—just for us."

After their long walk, the bears settled down for bed. "We are lucky," yawned Baby Bear. "Our love *is* all around us."

"It's in my heart and yours,"
smiled Mommy.
And the bears slept the
whole night through,
their hearts full of love.

To Autumn, may your world be full of love. xxx ~ D.M.

To Leo ~ S.B.

tiger tales

5 River Road, Suite 128, Wilton, CT 06897
Published in the United States 2020
Text by Danielle McLean
Text copyright © 2020 Little Tiger Press Ltd.
Illustrations copyright © 2020 Sebastien Braun
ISBN-13: 978-1-68010-194-2
ISBN-10: 1-68010-194-3
Printed in China
LTP/1800/2967/0919
All rights reserved
10 9 8 7 6 5 4 3 2 1

For more insight and activities, visit us at www.tigertalesbooks.com